FROM FAR AWAY

STORY BY ROBERT MUNSCH AND SAOUSSAN ASKAR

ART BY REBECCA GREEN

annick press
toronto + berkeley

We acknowledge the support of the Canada Council for the Arts and the Ontario Arts Council, and the participation of the Government of Canada/la participation du gouvernement du Canada for our publishing activities.

Cataloging in Publication

Munsch, Robert N., 1945–, author
    From far away / Robert Munsch, Saoussan Askar; Rebecca Green, illustrator.

Previously published: Toronto: Annick Press, 1995.
Previous edition illustrated by Michael Martchenko.

Issued in print and electronic formats.
ISBN 978-1-55451-940-8 (hardcover).—ISBN 978-1-55451-939-2 (softcover).—
ISBN 978-1-55451-942-2 (PDF).—ISBN 978-1-55451-941-5 (EPUB)
    1. Askar, Saoussan–Juvenile fiction. I. Askar, Saoussan, author II. Green, Rebecca, 1986–, illustrator III. Title.

PS8576.U575F76 2017   jC813'.54   C2017-901397-1
                                           C2017-901398-X

Published in the U.S.A. by Annick Press (U.S.) Ltd.
Distributed in Canada by University of Toronto Press.
Distributed in the U.S.A. by Publishers Group West.

Printed in China

Visit us at: annickpress.com
Visit Robert Munsch at: robertmunsch.com
Visit Rebecca Green at: myblankpaper.com

Also available in e-book format. Please visit www.annickpress.com/ebooks.html for more details. Or scan

To my beautiful homeland of Canada—may our land always be filled with love and light—S.A.

To Saoussan—R.M.

For my mother—R.G.

The place we used to live was very nice.
But then a war started.

"There's no food," my father said.

"We are getting shot at," my mother said.

Bombs made holes in the wall.

One day, a really big BOOM made our roof fall in.

"We have to leave," my father and mother said.

My father left first and was gone for a long time. Then a letter came with plane tickets to a new country. I didn't like the plane. It made me sick. Nobody wanted to sit near me.

In the new country, my father took me to school and left me there. He said, "Be good and listen to your teacher." I listened to my teacher, only I didn't know what she was saying because she did not talk right.

Other kids tried to talk to me, but I was not able to answer. I didn't speak English.

I had a buddy who showed me the school
and played with me at recess. But she didn't
understand when I tried to teach her a rock
game I knew from back home.

At first, I didn't know how to say, "I want to go to the washroom." So I crawled out the door when the teacher wasn't looking. When I came back, I waited outside the door until someone opened it. Then I crawled back to my desk.

Once, I crawled to the washroom and saw a paper skeleton in the hallway, only I did not know what it was. I thought the skeleton was evil. I thought that people were going to start shooting each other here. I screamed a very good scream.

Everybody came running. They thought someone was being killed in the bathroom. My teacher tried to tell me that the skeleton wasn't real. It was made of paper and was going to be used in the school play. I didn't understand. She jumped up and down and danced around to explain that the play was just for fun, but I thought the skeleton made her crazy and I screamed louder.

My teacher hugged me, just like my mother would. I didn't know how to say, "I'm so scared," but the big tear that went out of my eye said it for me.

I decided that the whole school was crazy and I did not want to stay there. But my father said I had to. He said that people here are not going to start shooting each other.

I had bad dreams about skeletons for a long time after that, but finally I began to talk, little by little. I learned enough English to make friends, and school started to be fun.

Now I am in grade two and I am the best reader and speller in the class. I read and write a lot of stories. The teacher is now complaining that I'm never quiet.

So far, my favorite part of grade two is the trip our class took to the zoo. We got to see the pandas and monkeys and eat pizza and nobody shot at us the whole time.

I decided that my new country is a nice place.
I changed my name from Saoussan to Susan,
but my mother told me to change it back.

My teacher moved from our school. I saw her in the mall once and ran to her and hugged her. She was my first teacher in this country and she helped me a lot.

Saoussan in 1995, when *From Far Away* was first published.

A Note from Saoussan Today

Writing and publishing this story made me realize how many people struggle with finding a place of their own and with being understood by those around them. I have had people from all walks of life share with me their own stories of struggle and integration.

This story was published when I was at Ellesmere Public School in Toronto, Ontario, Canada. I went on to complete my schooling in a bilingual program in Ontario. I received a Bachelor of Health Studies from York University in Toronto, Ontario, and I recently completed my Master of Arts in Sociology at McGill University in Montreal, Quebec. I continue to be an avid reader and a lover of new languages. The language I am currently working on learning is German, and next on my list is Hebrew. I currently reside in Montreal with my husband, and am planning on taking a trip around the world very soon.

—Saoussan, 2017